To JUDY

ENJOY...

the trashman

Grains of Sand

From the Beaches
of Hilton Head Island,
South Carolina

bob bredin
a.k.a. the trashman

To Pam

My Wife and Best Friend

Acknowledgements

*Many people have
contributed to the contents of
this book.
Too many to list.
Somewhere along the way
I hope I've thanked you all.*

*Cover and Design
Pam Bredin*

Contents

My Job as a Trashman

Hilton Head Island is a popular resort community, ringed by miles of sandy beaches and warm ocean waters. My job is to help keep that environment clean. I work for Hilton Head Beach Services. I am a trashman.

Each morning, my partner in litter, Bill and I set out to rid the sands of plastic bottles, flip-flops, potato chip bags, socks, rusted beach chairs, kids' pails, orange peels, juicy juice boxes, used pampers, hotel towels, kites hopelessly wrapped in tangled cord, beer cans, thongs, birthday balloons, sandwich bags, gnarly dog-eaten tennis balls, ketchup packets, pizza slices, and spent bottle rockets. Are you getting the picture here, people? The list is endless. If it's trash, we pick it, bag it, and haul it to the dump.

In addition, we're responsible for the proper burial of fish and wildlife that wash up on the shore: pelicans, turtles, stingrays, sharks, and even occasional alligators. But not jelly fish. Our operations manual clearly directs that God is responsible for removing dead jellies.

Our tour of duty starts at sunrise and continues until we have scrubbed the landscape of man's trash transgressions from the previous day.

Our territory is twelve miles of shoreline and includes the inspection of one hundred twenty barrels.

To carry out our mission, Bill and I drive a red truck, hitched to a ten-foot utility trailer, up and down the sands, while little kids wave excitedly. Growing up I often fantasized about a summer job driving an ice cream wagon and ringing the magical pied piper bell. I'm convinced this is as close as I'll ever get to the realization of that dream.

The Coligny Water Fountain

Our beach patrol day starts at Coligny Plaza, which is the entrance to the island's busiest beach. Three years ago the town invested three million dollars and gave the park a major facelift. Walkways made of exotic rosewood, and edged with oyster shell and brick, wind through floral gardens and ornamental grasses. Adirondack chairs and weathered benches give visitors a comfortable place to relax and view the beach. Even the men's and ladies' rooms are hidden beneath live oaks and disguised as tiny cottages with tropical shutters.

But the jewel of Coligny Plaza is the fountain that sends water plumes high into the air. On a hot summer day the park is filled with delighted children, laughing and running through the choreographed jet sprays. However, few tourists have read the Rules of Operation for the Park, which is tucked away amidst the ornamental grasses. The sign states: Persons with Diarrhea Shall Not Use the Fountain.

Every day, when I drive by the sign, I wonder whose ideas it was to discriminate against those poor souls with diarrhea. But then I am thankful Bill and I don't have to enforce that section of the beach conduct code.

Mysterious Lady

I saw a woman reading on the beach yesterday. She's been camped in the same spot all week. She wears a straw hat with floppy brim and oversized dark glasses. Her face is hidden from view, as is her body, wrapped in a blanket from the Holiday Inn. Her seated position never changes. Her knees are drawn up and used to support the book she's reading.

Twenty feet behind her is a trash barrel which I inspect daily. As I do, I look over and smile. She doesn't notice. She never moves or looks up. She is too engrossed in her book.

Today she's gone but has left me something. In the middle of her sand-streaked blanket is the book she had been reading...a Gideon's Bible, compliments of the Holiday Inn.

The Stingray

How the lifeguard managed to get the huge fish into the trailer, I'll never know. The stingray measured six feet long and was as wide as it was tall. Even lying dead on the trailer deck, it was an intimidating creature. Its menacing spiked tail, which could send bathers to the emergency room, was longer than my arm. Its beady, steel grey eyes, open even in death, seemed to follow me as I moved.

"Found it floating in the surf this morning," the tanned young lifeguard said matter-of-factly. "Looks like the sharks did a nasty on it."

Two large clumps of flesh were missing from both sides of the ray's head. The bites had been symmetrically delivered in an eight-inch arc. However, the greatest damage to the ray's wing and torso had been done from behind. Three massive bites, measuring more than a foot across, suggested there might have been a number of sharks involved in the attack.

"Need some help burying it?" I asked timidly, my eyes still fixed on the stingray's wounds.

"Nah, thanks" came the reply, as his truck started moving down the beach.

I stood there quietly for a minute, looking out over the waters, reflecting on what I had just witnessed. With the exception of a few small waves, the scene was calm and peaceful. However, my mind was thinking ahead a month to an ocean race that would have me swimming in these waters. The image of what those sharks had done to a six-foot stingray would remain with me for a while. But then I smiled, trying to remain positive. Maybe it would motivate me to swim faster.

The Chair

"Beach chair…ten o'clock." I muttered softly.

My partner, Bill, who was driving, nodded slightly and stopped the red truck midway between the chair and a plastic bottle.

It was near the end of our beach patrol shift, and the bright overhead sun had already drained us to the point where we were ready to call it a day. Bill headed for the bottle, while I trudged through soft sand towards the chair.

Our patrol routinely picks up a dozen chairs daily and hauls them to the dump. Most are old and broken, but a surprising number are new. They're usually bought the first day of vacation and left on the beach when the holiday ends.

This chair, however, belonged in the old-but-healthy category. It was heavy and well made, although rust had begun to claim parts of its metal frame. The original webbing had been white, but over the years, as pieces wore out, they had been replaced with strips of varied colors. None of the colors matched. The chair was facing the ocean, and a message had been neatly printed on its webbing. I read the inscription several times before calling Bill over.

In Memory of
Harriet Susan Marks
1/14/36 – 10/7/10
Best Mother Ever

"Are we going to take it to the dump?" I asked tentatively.

"I'm not," Bill said, clearing his throat.

That evening I Googled Harriet Susan Marks. I searched names, birth records, deaths, but found nothing. It was as if she never existed, except to the son or daughter who remembered her as...the best mother ever.

Bad Kite Day

It was raining today. A light steady rain accompanied by winds gusting off the ocean. The beach was deserted, except for a middle-aged man dressed in full yellow rain gear, accompanied by a small boy in a bathing suit and wearing swim goggles. The dramatic difference in their dress gave the pair a comical appearance. The man was trying to get a kite airborne, while shouting instructions to the boy.

"Now Ben, hold the string tight and don't let go. I'll tell you when."

"Okay Dad, I'm ready," the boy replied confidently. But he started running too soon, and the kite nosedived onto the hard sand.

It was clearly not kite flying weather, but somehow it struck me that this father and son combination would have difficulty, no matter what the weather. They tried several more launches with similar results. Finally I heard the father call an end to the exercise.

"C'mon son. We have to go. It's getting late."

Silently the boy retrieved the kite and handed it to his father, who was now on his cell phone. The boy stood patiently, head down, poking at the sand with his toe.

When the man finished his conversation, his attention turned back to the boy. He ran his hand through the boy's long, wet hair, and then put an arm around his shoulder. He tried to make eye contact as he talked, but the boy refused to look up.

As I sat in the red truck, I wondered what the father was saying. Was he sorry he waited till their last day of vacation before flying the kite? Was he promising to spend more time with his son? And the boy, I wondered if he understood any of the pressures his father was under.

Finally the two walked off the beach, but not together.

The Chair (continued)

Bill and I checked out the Harriet Susan Mark's chair today. It was still in the same spot. I wonder who she was, and what kind of life she led? Who put the chair on the beach and why? Was it a child, or perhaps a grandchild, who could not bear the thought of the chair ending up at the dump? And who printed "best mother ever" on the webbing and set it on the beach looking out over the ocean?

The Wedding

It was still dark. Morning had not yet broken as red truck #6 pulled onto Coligny Beach.

"Do you think the sun will rise today, Bill?" I asked tongue-in-check.

"Bet on it" he offered, ignoring my sarcasm. Then looking at his watch added, "In exactly fourteen minutes."

"Why do you do that, Bill?" I asked.

"Do what?"

"Memorize sunrise times."

Bill started a lengthy explanation in response to my question, but I had turned him off. In the rear mirror I was watching a woman in a flowing white wedding dress make her way down the beach. As she passed my window I called out, "Looks like it's gonna be a good day."

"Oh yes," she smiled, "A very good day."

Holding her arm tightly was a man I guessed was her father. He wore a blue blazer with tan slacks and tugged at the tie around his neck. They both were having difficulty walking in the soft sand.

"Where are they going?" I whispered softly to Bill as they passed the truck.

"There," he said, pointing to a spot up the beach where five white chairs had been set up.

"Not a very big wedding. That's a long walk in the sand," I added. "Maybe we should offer them a ride."

"Yeah," Bill laughed. "We'll put them in the trailer with the trash. Good way to start a marriage."

Five minutes later the ceremony was over, and, as the small group hugged and kissed by the water's edge, a magnificent red sun peeked above the horizon. The darkness retreated, and a new day full of hope and promise had begun.

The Book of Knowledge

At the conclusion of each beach patrol shift, Bill makes entries in a small spiral notebook he calls the Book of Knowledge. The title is misleading because the notes refer to the location and description of beach umbrellas, chairs, and canopies that were removed and taken to the dump in accordance with town ordinance 8-1-211.

The town of Hilton Head has a policy that no beach paraphernalia can be left on the sands overnight. If it is, the beach patrol, specifically Bill and I, tag it on Day One, tag it again on Day Two, and finally, on Day Three throw it in the red trailer and haul it to the dump.

It's a lot of paperwork for a rusted beach chair whose owner is now back at work in Ohio.

Sister Nike

"She's back," Bill observed as he emptied a load of trash into the trailer. "We haven't seen her in a couple of weeks."

"Who?" I asked.

"Sister Nike." He nodded towards a nun walking down by the water's edge. Dressed in a full black habit, she was easy to spot. It was barley eight a.m., but the humidity had already reached an uncomfortable level.

"She must be roasting in that outfit. I thought Catholic Nuns gave up habits years ago and started wearing street clothes."

"Well, apparently someone forgot to tell Sister Nike," Bill chuckled. "Looks like she's finished her morning devotions and is in to the power phase of her walk."

The Sister's routine seldom varied. First came morning devotions; with head bowed and hands folded across her chest, she slowly walked the sands. If you were close enough, you could she her fingering the beads. This was followed by her power walk, and it was how she earned the nickname Sister Nike. As her pace increased, she would begin pumping her arms, and the motion lifted the hem of her robe enough to reveal bright pink exercise shoes.

I once asked Bill if he thought the good Sister was under contract to Nike. Those modern athletic shoes peeking out from beneath the black robe would have made a good commercial.

Usually Sister Nike's morning ritual lasted exactly an hour, and she was gone. That's why we were surprised to see her, at the end of our shift, still on the beach. She was sitting cross-legged on the sands, engrossed in conversation with a stunningly attractive, deeply tanned woman. The contrast between the two was dramatic. Sister Nike clothed in black; her friend in a skimpy silver bikini. The Sister was smiling, and I wondered what the bikini lady was telling her.

One Shoe Off / One Shoe On

It shouldn't surprise anyone to learn a lot of footwear is left on the beach: everything from cheap flip-flops to designer sandals. What is surprising is that they are rarely left in pairs. How does someone lose just one shoe? It's one of the great debates amongst trashmen.

Footwear is worn in pairs and taken off in pairs. Why then do we find so many individual flip-flops adrift on the sand?

And when you arrive home with only "one-shoe-on", what do you do with it? Keep it in your closet, hoping that one day you'll find the missing mate?

The Chair (continued)

I've visited the Best Mother Chair each day this week. It hasn't been tagged for removal yet, but I know its time on the beach is limited.

Eating Ice Cream on a Hot Day

I smiled as I watched him walk past. His gaze was fixed on the melting ice cream cone he held protectively with both hands. He had light brown skin, dark wavy hair, and a trimmed mustache. His neatly pressed cotton shirt complemented his tan linen slacks, and his expensive leather sandals were not the type usually seen on the beach. He had a definite European air.

It was late morning, and, despite the sea breeze, the temperature had already climbed into the mid-nineties, sending rivulets of vanilla cream down the sides of the cone he was juggling.

I watched in amusement as the man struggled to stop the flow with his tongue, but it was evident he had never eaten ice cream under these conditions. His technique of repeatedly jabbing at the melting ball with outstretched tongue was humorous, but ineffective. Soon his hands were covered with the white liquid, then his mustache, and finally the tip of his nose.

By now several bystanders were watching the drama unfold, and the man, sensing he was providing entertainment for others, flashed a weak smile, bowed apologetically to no one in particular, and tossed what was left of the vanilla ice cream cone into a nearby trash barrel.

Charles Schultz once wrote in his Peanuts comic strip, "Life is an ice cream cone. You have to lick it one day at a time."

The Devil's Darning Needle

They're back. I saw two or three today. Tomorrow they'll be more. And before the month is over they'll be thousands. I remember several days last season when they filled the air, and it was impossible to move without one of the creatures smacking into your head. Dragonflies have a sinister look, with large bulbous eyes and double wings. Hilton Head is one of their migratory stops.

When I was a kid, my Mother referred to them as the "Devil's Darning Needle" and warned, if I spoke disrespectfully to my elders, they would sew my lips together. I believed her. Now, many years later, my heart beats a little faster each time one of those monster bugs flies near my face.

Finders Keepers

I have a recurring dream that dates back to my adolescent years. I'm walking on a crowded city sidewalk, being careful not to step on any cracks and break my old man's back. People are coming towards me, but because I'm looking down, I see only the lower half of their bodies and not their faces. At some point in my dream I step off the curb and continue walking in the gutter. The crowd and the sidewalk cracks disappear, making my journey easier. Then, up ahead, I see two pennies partially buried in the dirt. I stoop to pick them up, and in so doing spot a nickel... and then a dime. Eventually I find a quarter. The faster I move, the more coins I discover.

It's a wonderful dream that always ends too soon… usually before I have collected more than a dollar.

Today, as I emptied a trash barrel on the beach, I discovered a ten-dollar bill partially buried in the sand. For a long moment I thought I was experiencing my old recurring dream, but I wasn't.

Sometimes dreams do come true.

The Chair (continued)

There were two violation tags when I stopped by the Best Mother chair today. I looked up and down the beach to make certain no one was watching, before ripping off the tags and hiding the chair behind another dune.

Mother's Day is next week. I hope the chair can make it.

Patriotism

A lot of American values have changed in the past decade. Patriotism is one. Recent surveys indicate many citizens believe there are better countries to live in than America. Many have forgotten the words to the National Anthem.

Today I met a patriotic man on the beach. He was surf fishing, and between his two fishing rods was a bamboo pole flying a gigantic American flag. Although it was barely dawn, I saw the ensign flapping in the morning breeze half a mile away. The sun had just risen. The man was alone. No one else was there to bear witness.

I wanted to stop and shake his hand, but didn't. Something held me back. I drove by slowly. But a quarter-mile down the beach, I stopped the truck, got out, stood as straight as I could, and saluted.

XXX-Rated

"Is that what I think it is?" Bill asked, his voice a mix of amusement and disbelief.

He was pointing at a sand sculpture, but not one normally seen on family beaches. It was the male and female genitalia. However, the male's anatomy was proportionately larger and in much greater detail than the female's, leading me to the conclusion they were crafted by different artists.

As the discussion continued, it became apparent Bill and I both needed a refresher course in Anatomy 101, so we shifted the conversation to the fate of the XXX-rated sculptures.

Bill, always the conservative, argued because Hilton Head is a family beach, the work needs to be destroyed. It simply was not suitable viewing for young children. I argued for freedom of expression, adding it was not our job to judge what constitutes pornography

In the end Bill, with his job seniority, won out, and I was dispatched with a shovel to spread both reproductive organs back across the sands.

Good News on the Radio

The red truck is equipped with a short wave radio that is on during morning patrol. For the most part it's chatter between base headquarters and the lifeguards concerning equipment. But every now and then something significant is broadcast, such as a shark sighting, medical emergency, or swimmer in distress.

It was at the end of our shift today, and I was washing the truck when this broadcast came across: "Attention all stations- Chair #143 at the Westin Hotel is reporting a lost child. Missing approximately five minutes. Last seen at water's edge in front of the hotel. The boy, who is four, answers to the name of Michael. He's wearing a green bathing suit. All stations acknowledge."

My thoughts flashed back to the beach that morning. The sands were hot and crowded, and the surf invitingly high. Had four year old Michael been lured into the ocean?

I waited a minute...two minutes...three... not good I thought.

And then the radio crackled: "All stations this net - missing boy has been found".

I breathed deeply and went back to washing the red truck.

The Crows

Two black crows were perched on the edge of a trash barrel, both cawing loudly. As I approached the barrel, their attention shifted to me. Was it my imagination, or were they becoming more aggressive? I looked up and down the beach, quickly counting two dozen more crows. Where had the seagulls gone, I wondered, and when had the crows taken over their domain? Were they now the scavengers of the beach?

That evening I Googled "Crows on the Beach" and discovered a blog written six months earlier by a woman living in Southern California. She claimed the crows were taking over the sands where she lived too.

"This is wrong," I thought as I read her story. Crows belong in cornfields: seagulls belong on the beach.

Later the next day, I saw a lone seagull perched on one leg by the water's edge. Its feathers were ruffled, as if it had just been in a fight, and its head sagged wearily to one side. As I got closer, it tried to fly away but could only manage a series of short hops.

The Crows (continued)

On our patrol today we saw only two gulls, while again the crows were everywhere. It reminded me of the scene from Alfred Hitchcock's movie, in which the birds took over a small New England town and started attacking people.

Bill told me he recently saw three crows chasing a hawk. He thinks it has something to do with global warming.

New Clothes

You meet lots of interesting people on the beach. Many are "regulars." Gordon's an example.

He rarely talks with anyone, except us. His walk is slow and deliberate, as if the act itself is painful. Each day he wears the same faded gray t-shirt and Boston Red Sox baseball hat.

One day I suggested, "Gordon, you need to get some new walking duds. Something befitting a man of your stature."

"Really? Like what?" he asked.

"Leave it to us," I replied.

For the next week we culled dozens of discarded, dump-bound shirts, until we found the perfect one hanging from a dune fence. It was a homemade, tie-dye creation, rich with psychedelic colors. It was so "not-Gordon": it was perfect.

The next day we wrapped our gift in a white plastic trash bag and presented it to him, along with a few words about how we valued his friendship. For a moment I thought he was going to cry. For two weeks it was the only shirt he wore.

Later, we saw him talking with a much younger, very attractive woman.

No-see-ums

They're known by many different names: biting midges, sand fleas, gnats, and steel teeth. Here in the low country we call them no-see-ums, because they're barely visible to the human eye. But those tiny critters, a third the size of a mosquito, pack a monstrous bite. Peter Frost, writing in the Island Packet newspaper recently, compared the two insects as follows: "Unlike mosquitoes, which extract blood with a needle-like probe, no-see-ums use piercing, rasping teeth that slash the skin to get their meal."

Like most biting insects, they are attracted to carbon dioxide in respiration and lactic acid in perspiration. Those who perspire more, and breathe more heavily, attract more biting insects.

When it's no-see-um season on Hilton Head, swarms of the steel teeth critters are everywhere. And if you step on a pile of seaweed and disturb a nest, bug spray isn't going to protect you. That's because they attack in a horde, with the same bug biting multiple times.

And one last cautionary note: if you're in a red truck going 15 mph down the beach, you can't outrun 'em either.

Engineers at Work

Have you ever watched an engineer put something together? Today I observed while three engineers attempted to set up two beach canopies. The position of the sun, the direction of the wind, the view of the water, and support for the structure itself, were all part of their deliberations. It took four hours, and two cases of beer to complete the task.

Their wives were noticeably absent.

Aqua Cycle Rescue at Sea

Bill and I had to rescue two Aqua Cycles from the surf today. An Aqua Cycle is an adult version of a kid's big wheel that floats on water. Beach Services rents them to vacationers, although they're not a popular item.

Last night someone stole two of the big plastic toys and took them for an ocean joyride.

"Whoever did this must have been high on something," I said to Bill, as we watched the two red and yellow bikes wallow in the surf.

"Yeah, top speed on one of those blimps can't be more than a mile an hour. Not my idea of a thrilling ride."

"What are we gonna do?" I asked. At crucial times like this I've learned it's best to have the boss make the decisions.

"Well, the tide's going out," Bill reasoned. "If we don't get them now, by noon they will be in Port Royal Sound."

We waded into the ocean together and quickly discovered that rescuing an Aqua Cycle bobbing in rolling surf requires a degree of dexterity which neither Bill nor I had.

If someone had been there to film our efforts, however, I'm sure it would have made an entertaining You-Tube video.

Gloomy Weather

It was a gloomy day on the beach – damp and cold with the threat of rain. The Island Packet Newspaper, under their weather forecast, called it "a perfect day for a nap."

And so… that afternoon… I took their advice.

My Solo Cup Collection

I collect 16-ounce solo drinking cups that have been discarded on the beach. My good wife, Pam, thinks it's silly and makes me keep them in the garage, even though they don't take up much room. I have red, pink, purple, black, brown, and white cups. In addition, various shaded cups of yellow, green, and blue. I'm still searching the sands for the rare gold and silver species needed to complete my collection.

I know I could buy them at a party supply store, but that's not the type of collector I am.

Every Now and Then a Surprise

Because I spend most of the morning with my head down, looking for stuff that doesn't belong on the beach, every now and then I get rewarded with something besides a plastic bottle.

Earlier this year I found a soggy twenty-dollar bill tucked into a Camels cigarette pack and, last month, a pair of designer sunglasses. However, today's find was unique by any standard. It was a light bulb. Not the General Electric 100 watt variety, but a really big light bulb. It was nearly three feet long and two feet in circumference. I thought it was large enough to have come from a lighthouse. But where? And if it was a navigational bulb, how did it end up in the ocean?

On the way home I decided I'd give it to my ten-year-old grandson, Nathaniel, and suggest he write a story about a lighthouse swallowed by the sea. Or perhaps it's not a bulb from a lighthouse. Maybe it's part of the communications system from an alien spaceship, and the aliens are desperately looking to recover it.

Healthy Fish

Most of the people who fish in the waters surrounding Hilton Head Island are environmentally responsible with their trash. But every now and then someone leaves a cardboard bait box behind. Today I retrieved two from the beach and made an interesting discovery: a listing of nutritional facts on the back on the box.

My immediate reaction was, "Nutritional data for fish bait? Whose bright idea was this?"

But there it was: a four-ounce serving of bait contained 110 calories and two grams of fat.

While that was good, the cholesterol count was alarming: 260 milligrams, or 87% of a fish's daily requirement.

"How did we compute a cholesterol measurement for a fish?" I asked myself.

By the time I reached the red truck I was laughing out loud.

"What's so funny?" Bill asked.

I shoved the smelly bait box under his nose. "The world is getting nuttier by-the-day. Read this."

Bill was quiet for a moment and then said reflectively, "I hope the fish don't see this. It will hurt the industry."

Love Letters in the Sand

Beachgoers have always enjoyed writing messages in the sand. Forty years ago I recall expressing my undying love for Pam Norton on the shores of Buzzards Bay at low tide, proclaiming for all to see "B.B. & P.N." inside a lopsided heart.

Today's sand scripts remain outpourings of the soul, but they've become much more graphic and are often used to express love gone bad: "I don't love you anymore, Joey. You're an asshole."

The Ballerina

There was no sunrise to view this morning over Coligny. The low-hanging, puffy clouds blocked it out. But that did not stop a ballerina who danced and twirled over the hard beach sands.

Those who came to witness a sunrise were not disappointed. The ballerina quickly took center stage, as she leapt and spiraled for her audience. While she danced, the beach became silent. Two dogs paused in their pursuit of shorebirds. A jogger pushing a baby carriage stopped.   Even a lone ghost crab became motionless as the dancer glided past.

When the ballerina finished, the sun showed its approval by peeking out from behind a cloud, and I headed for the nearest trash barrel, with a smile and a light step.

Beach Marker #26

They had another party at beach marker #26 last night. The brown condo complex seems to be a favorite with the younger vacation crowd. The revelers did a decent job cleaning up after the party, but some paper stuff still wound up in the dunes. That's where I was when I picked up a red, plastic cup. The clear black print against the red background made the message stand out.

"I'm not yours. Put me back." It was in a woman's script.

I showed it to Bill when I got back to the truck. "What do you think she's saying?" I asked.

"She's trying to prevent someone from taking her drink by mistake," Bill said matter-of-factly.

"I don't think so," I countered, placing the cup in my trash bucket. "I think she's in a bad relationship with some guy, but doesn't know how to get out of it. He's trying to control her, and she wants it to end."

Bill got that you-gotta-be-kidding look on his face, then asked sarcastically, "So she writes, 'I'm not yours. Put me back.' on her rum and coke cup. Is that how you see it?"

"Yeah. Well it's a little more lady-like than, 'I don't love you anymore. You're an asshole.' Isn't it?"

The White Ibis

Bill maneuvered the red truck down by the water's edge so I could have a closer look. He told me he'd seen this sight many times before, but it was a first for me.

A white ibis was waiting patiently, less than ten feet from a fisherman who was surf fishing. The bird remained motionless while the man fished, but as soon it heard the click of the reel and the line being retrieved, it cocked its head slightly to one side, anticipating what might happen next.

"Where'd the bird learn that?" I whispered in Bill's direction.

"Beats me," he replied with a smile. "I guess at some point a fisherman threw him a fish, and the bird remembered. It's probably easier panhandling for meals on the beach, than spending the day traipsing about a muddy lagoon."

I knew Bill was joking, but later that evening, I wondered about the white ibis and it's new lifestyle. I wondered how long the bird had been fishing this way. Was panhandling really easier? And more importantly, if the white ibis was now on a modified food stamp program, could the blue heron be far behind?

Mr. Marshall at Starbucks

It was raining today, with winds gusting to thirty knots, so Bill and I stopped for coffee at Starbucks before heading to the beach. We usually save Starbuck's coffee for special occasions like bad weather, when we're forced to chase the trash.

The store had just opened, and the only person in line was a stooped, arthritic gentleman, whom I thought should be home in bed, not out in this weather. It was hard to guess his age. He might have been sixty, but looked ninety. As a young man I'm sure he was a six-footer, but time and arthritis had taken its toll. His large head drooped forward, while his shoulders sagged around a sunken chest. A little potbelly extended over his pants, and his skinny legs bowed out, accenting knobby knees.

He had a breathing apparatus clipped to his belt, with the plastic tube winding upward into his nose. Except for several strands of wispy, white hair, he was bald, but smartly dressed in a collared shirt with matching polo shorts.

He waited patiently, his eyes fixed on the counter, until the barista came with his order.

"Here you are, Mr. Marshall", she said pleasantly. "Your veni mocha macchiato and sticky cinnamon"… Her voice trailed off describing the gooey pastry that went with the man's special coffee. He handed her a plastic card, she swiped it, and then assisted him as he shuffled out the door.

"Must be a regular customer," I said when she returned.

"Yep, every day, except Sunday. Same thing."

As Bill and I left the store we passed a '65 Cadillac Eldorado, with the big fins, parked in the lot. It was in mint condition, with the rain beaded on a well-waxed finish. The headlights and several interior lights were on, while Mr. Marshall enjoyed his 6:00 a.m. breakfast.

"Not a bad way to start a rainy day," I said to Bill as we headed for the red truck.

"Yeah," he replied, "Did you see that pastry? It must have been at least 2000 calories. I wish I could eat one of those every day. Mr. Marshall sure is living the good life."

How Does He Do That?

Jack's a lifeguard at beach marker #28. He's a muscular six-footer with washboard abs. You can't pinch his stomach because there's no loose skin there.

I saw Jack at a local diner Saturday having a late breakfast. His plate was piled with scrambled eggs, home fries, bacon, sausage, and toast.

As I sat unnoticed on a nearby stool sipping my coffee, the grill man delivered a separate order of hot cakes and another side of bacon. Jack drenched both in maple syrup.

For the next few minutes I amused myself by calculating on a napkin how many calories were being consumed in this food orgy. Assuming the three large cokes that accompanied the meal were not sugar-free, my best guess is around four thousand.

Did I mention Jack has zero body fat?

Do the Jelly Fish Sting?

I was standing on the trailer hitch, putting a liner in a trash barrel, when I heard a young voice ask, "Hey Mister, do these jelly fish sting?"

I stepped down and smiled at the skinny, freckled kid, who was looking up at me while shielding his eyes from the bright sun. He was no more than eight and wearing a bathing suit several sizes too large.

Before I had an opportunity to answer, he turned and pointed to a young teenager standing at the water's edge, holding a boogie board and smiling.

"My brother said if you pee on the jelly fish bite, it won't sting. Is that true, mister, or is he lying?"

"Well, the jellies you see on this beach are called cannon balls," I said, launching into my jellyfish 101 lecture, "and they've lost their tentacles at sea so they can't sting." I started to explain how this takes place, but saw the boy had lost interest.

"Did something in the water sting you?" I asked, shifting gears.

"Nah, I don't think so…well, maybe a little," he said, turning and running off to join his brother.

"Thanks mister," he shouted over his shoulder.

And I was left to wonder, if I had told the boy, "Yes. Urine is a remedy for jelly stings," would he have let his big brother pee on him?

Defending a Ghost Crab

As we pulled onto the sands, my eyes focused on the three barrels overflowing with trash. Bill, however, was watching a teenage boy by the water's edge prodding a ghost crab with a stick.

I was startled though when he shouted out the truck window, "Hey…Don't do that!"

There was no reaction from the boy.

"Excuse me. Please, leave the crab alone," Bill repeated as he maneuvered the red truck closer.

Up to this point the boy's focus was on the crab. Now he looked up. His expression was a mixture of meanness and contempt. Then, without saying a word, he returned to poking the crab, but with a greater vengeance.

Bill grabbed the portable walkie-talkie as he jumped from the truck. By now the boy was thrashing the nearly dead shellfish.

"I said don't do that," Bill ordered, only louder this time.

This one got the boy's attention. He shot back, "What's the hell's the matter with you? It's a God damn crab." Bill put the walkie-talkie to his mouth, and in a quieter, but stern voice demanded, "This is the last time I'm going to warn you. Stop or I'll call the police."

By now, less than six feet separated the two, and the boy was holding the pointed stick like a sword aimed at Bill's chest. Sensing the situation was getting out of hand I spoke up.

"Listen, if the police come, you're the one who'll be in trouble." I guessed he was on vacation, and added, "You'll spend the day in a cell at the police station. It's not worth it."

The boy was silent for a moment but continued staring at Bill. Finally he threw the stick in our direction, muttered something I didn't understand, and strode off towards the Holiday Inn.

Too Many Straws

"I hate straws," Bill fumed, as he emptied his bucket.

"Ya, I know…me, too," I replied.

"They're everywhere," he continued, "Clear straws, colored straws, bent straws. They're taking over the beach."

"Ya, I know," I repeated. Bill was on a roll, and I knew better than to interrupt him. Besides, it was Monday morning, and the sands bore the scars of all those weekend beach goers.

"I read somewhere recently about a kid in Vermont who's trying to get straws outlawed. That kid's sure got my vote," Bill continued, shaking his head.

"Come on, I know there's a bunch of radicals parading around the Green Mountain State, but how do you get straws outlawed?" I asked. Sometimes I enjoy baiting Bill, and this was one of those times.

The next morning, as I expected, Bill had all the answers to how it was being done.

"His name's Milo Cress. He's called the straw kid, and he's only nine years old. Bet you didn't know this," Bill announced, regurgitating his Google research. "There are approximately five hundred million disposable straws used every day in this country. That's enough to fill 9300 school buses. Amazing stuff, huh?"

Before I could answer, Bill took off again.

"But this is one smart 4th grader. What he's doing is simply urging all restaurant owners to stop making straws an automatic accessory with beverages. He wants them first to ask if the customer wants a straw. Apparently he's already gotten a number of the McDonald's Restaurants in Burlington to buy into the program. It's a win-win situation for everyone."

"We could use Milo here on Hilton Head," I interrupted.

Later that morning I reflected further on Milo's accomplishments. All I could remember doing in the 4th grade was pulling the pigtails of the little girl who sat in front of me.

Saving a Salamander

It's my day off, yet here I am on the beach sipping my Dunkin Donuts coffee. I often come to the beach when I have a problem or just want to think about things.

The sun has just made a spectacular entrance, splashing the clouds in peach colored hues, but leaving the sky creamy white.

I watch a salamander scurry towards me, and for the moment forget why I came to the beach. What's a salamander doing here on the sand? There's no food supply. There's no place to hide. He doesn't belong.

The salamander cocks his head to one side and looks up. He's speaking to me. He doesn't move when I gently pick him up and carry him off the beach.

Dream Interpretation

Bill told me he had a dream last night. Dreams are one of the subjects we frequently discuss in the truck. Both of us dream regularly, but rarely agree on their interpretation. Bill's one of the few people I know who has happy dreams, so, when he told me this one was a nightmare, I was surprised. Even more so when I learned it was a beach patrol dream and I was in it.

"Well," he started slowly, "We'd had a busy day, and the trailer was filled with trash, but not ordinary stuff. This load was really foul-smelling garbage. Lots of soiled pampers and vile liquids. The flies were everywhere…"

"Okay, stop! I get the picture," I interrupted.

"And you ordered me to ride in the trailer," Bill continued.

"What?" I blurted out.

"You ordered me to ride in the trailer with all that disgusting garbage," Bill repeated.

"Why'd I do that?"

"I don't know. You just did."

"And you did it? You crawled into that mess?" By now I was beginning to really enjoy Bill's dream. "Okay, then what happened?"

"I woke up."

"What?" I blurted out again, disappointed at the abrupt ending.

"I told you. I woke up."

"That's all there is to the dream?"

"Yeah. What do you think it means?"

For I moment I hesitated. I was enjoying the situation too much for it to end. So, I pretended I hadn't heard the question.

"What do I think it means?" I repeated thoughtfully, turning my good ear in Bill's direction.

And he repeated, louder and more distinctly, "Yeah. What do you think it means?"

"Well, the meaning is obvious," I said, trying not to smile. "You see me as a threat to your job security. You recognize me as a superior trashman, and the dream is a Freudian manifestation of your inner inability to cope with..."

"Enough. Enough," Bill shouted. "Right now I'd rather be in the trailer, submerged in garbage, than listening to your stupid babble."

"Careful now Bill," I warned. "You know dreams are the windows of men's souls, and right now your dreams don't smell so good."

Where's the Truant Officer

Hilton Head is not known as a surfing town. The waves are too small. There's a surf shop hidden at the south end of the island, but it sells more skim boards than surfboards

Nevertheless, every few months a storm at sea succeeds in raising four-foot waves at the beach, and the waters suddenly come alive with teenagers.

This past week was an example of that, when a Class 2 hurricane skirted the coast. On Monday, I counted more than fifty surfers in the water, and as the week progressed, I began to recognize a number of the faces. Then it dawned on me: most of these kids were playing hooky!

I remember once when I was in the 9th grade playing hooky to go sledding, after a nor'easter dropped more than three feet of snow. I was upset that school was not cancelled, and a buddy and I decided to protest the decision and spend the day sledding.

Somehow my Mother found out and threatened to report me to the school Truant Officer. I've forgotten his real name, but everyone called him Sgt. Greasy because of his hair.

I don't think we have truant officers in schools anymore. They've been replaced by armed police officers with metal detectors and search dogs.

Lots of things have changed since I was a young lad, but apparently kids still play hooky.

The Armadillo

We found a dead armadillo on the beach today. With its thick armored body, it looks like a prehistoric creature. According to Bill, there aren't supposed to be any on the island.

"How do you think it got here?" I asked.

"It has the same options we have," Bill replied. "Either it walked across the bridge or swam the channel." We both agreed it must have been the bridge, since neither of us thought the armadillo could swim.

"It's built like a tank," Bill insisted. "How can it swim? It had to walk across the bridge at night."

But just to be certain, I did some armadillo research that evening. The next morning I shared my findings with my unlearned colleague.

"While one might think the weight of the armadillo's shell would cause it to sink in the water, that is not the case," I started. "The animal has a unique ability to float by filling its lungs and stomach with air, causing it to swell to double its size. In addition it can hold its breath underwater for up to six minutes."

Bill remained silent, so I continued. "It is also interesting to note that, based on species, the female can delay her gestation period from three months to three years."

"Why would she want to do that?"

"Stress my boy...stress. Remarkable, huh? A mommy armadillo can control the birthing process from three months to three years."

Bill fell silent again, and I continued. "And during the 40's, derogatory references to armadillos as Hoover's hogs became common after the President failed to deliver on his promise of a chicken in every pot. I guess people started eating armadillo"

"Enough," Bill moaned, "If we ever find another dead armadillo, you're burying it."

My Daddy

I drove by a little girl on the beach today. She could have been seven, or eight, or maybe nine. Nowadays it's hard to tell. She was kneeling and had just finished writing on the hard sand with a stick. The letters were large and easy to read: " My Daddy is a liar."

Someone once said, "Life is a drawing, without an eraser." Maybe so, but in four hours, the incoming tide will give everyone a chance to start over.

Missing A Head

When I returned to beach patrol headquarters today, the five-gallon pail used for washing the red truck had an enormous skull in it. The pail was 3/4's filled with cloudy water, so just the top of the skull and one eye socket were visible. Slipping three fingers into the eye opening, I cautiously lifted the ghostly head. When the teeth became visible, I stopped. The pointed canines were two inches long. Dozens of smaller teeth were set irregularly in the jaw. Many were broken.

I quickly lowered the skull back into the bucket.

What kind of creature had this been? It wasn't an alligator or shark. The eye sockets were too big. And it couldn't have been a land animal because of the long, extended jaw.

It looked like a creature from another planet. Yet no one in the garage knew anything about it, or how it got there.

The following day it was gone.

Batman and Robin to the Rescue

It was a blustery morning. A gust of wind blew the truck door shut just as Bill shouted something back in my direction. He was kneeling on the sand, hidden from view by the truck's fender.

I recognized the words, "Oh my God," as Bill jumped up and, with outstretched arms, took off towards the ocean. He was carrying something in his hands. In the three years I'd worked with him, I had never seen Bill move that fast before.

"What's the matter?" I called out, but he didn't answer. By the time I caught up he was kneeling in the water, trying to untangle a wad of fishing line the size of a baseball. Peaking out of the knotted mess was the head of a baby loggerhead turtle.

"I don't know if it's still alive. It's not moving," Bill said, still breathless from his run. "It's a miracle I saw it. I thought I was just picking up a mess of tangled line."

We both worked with a sense of urgency for several minutes, until the newborn was free. Then Bill bent down and gently placed the tiny creature in the water. Immediately the shell began to sink.

"I think it's dead," I said, looking over at Bill. For a long time nothing happened, and then slowly a few bubbles emerged from inside the shell, followed by a baby head. Next came one flipper, and then another. Bill let out a proud father cheer, as his protégé bobbed to the surface and started swimming. More calls of encouragement followed as the newborn navigated a series of small waves.

We were both so involved in the magic of the event we didn't see the danger in the sky above. The seagull was already into its dive when I yelled. It was a loud, guttural scream that caught Bill unprepared. He spun around, lost his balance, and fell backwards into the water. The commotion halted the bird's attack. It hovered, flapping it's wings furiously, unsure whether to pursue the hunt, or look for easier prey. I continued my barrage of shouts as I waved my arms frantically. By now Bill had joined me.

Our defense proved too much for the gull. It decided the baby turtle, while a delectable morsel, was not worth the price of dealing with two deranged humans.

As the bird flew off we gave one last yelp, did an old man's version of a hi-five, and headed back for the truck. Good had triumphed over evil… or so we thought.

"Nice job, Batman," I said to Bill, reaching out and putting an arm around his shoulder.

"Couldn't have done it without you Robin." We both laughed.

Bill started the truck, and we sat there reliving the story. Then out of the corner of my eye, I saw a familiar shape returning from down the beach.

"Oh Lord...he's coming back!" Before the last words were out of my mouth, Bill had shifted into low gear and gunned the gas. The red truck lurched forward, throwing a rooster tail of sand out from the back tires.

The gull was now flying in small circles twenty feet offshore. Bill began punching the truck horn, as we sped towards the ocean. We were in a foot of seawater when he finally slammed on the brakes, creating a miniature tsunami.

Once again our rescue efforts proved successful. The gull flashed us a final evil eye and retreated out to sea.

I've heard it said the best portion of a person's life consists of those little nameless acts of kindness done for others. And that for me, includes baby logger head turtles

Beach Cycle Of Life

It all happened suddenly. Monday the beach was fine, but Tuesday millions of the tiny creatures appeared from nowhere. Sand fleas, or "no-see-ums" as the locals call them – minuscule, bloodsucking insects impervious to all brands of bug repellent. The vacationers slapped and scratched, but many gave up and left the beach.

Then on Wednesday, as if in answer to an SOS, the dragonflies descended. Only a few at first, but by midday Thursday the air was thick with them. They were everywhere – blue florescent creatures with large, bulbous eyes, and four wings allowing them to change direction instantly. They were eating machines, feasting on the smaller bugs. By the end of the day the windshield of the red truck was plastered with insect body parts.

But on Friday, once again, the roles reversed; the shore birds became the new hunters, and the dragon flies the hunted. Terns left the water's edge. Even brown pelicans joined the hunt.

Then on Sunday the cycle ended as quickly as it had started. The no-see-ums and the dragonflies were no more. The shore birds returned to the water and life on the beach went back to normal.

Do You Really Care?

I was putting a plastic liner in a barrel when a voice from behind startled me: "Good morning, and how are you this fine day?"

I turned, but the voice moved past me before I could respond. The voice was on its way for a brisk morning walk. I watched as it moved out of sight, and wondered what had prompted it to inquire how I was.

Did it care? A lot of chatter takes place today between people who really aren't interested in hearing your answer.

Traveler's Warning

It was low tide, and the flatness of the hard beach sand seemed to stretch forever. I stopped by a lone flip-flop that broke the beach's symmetry, and smiled at the message someone had written.

"Life is a journey. Wear comfortable shoes."

I thought about the warning and the sandal lying next to it, then picked up a broken shell and added a postscript.

"If it's going to be a long journey, wear two shoes."

It's Not Polite to Stare

I saw a man walking on the beach today wearing a tight-fitting Speedo bathing suit. He was tall and slender with little body fat, and his olive skin was smooth and unblemished. His graying hairs made me guess he was in his mid-fifties. As he walked, the exaggerated swing of his hips and arms resembled that of a runway model. With a hairpiece and makeup, he would have been an attractive woman, except for one thing: the bulge that protruded from the front of his swimsuit. It was dramatic.

"It's not polite to stare," Bill said, punching my arm.

"I'm not sure it's polite to go out in public dressed like that," I countered, continuing to stare.

"Would you say the same thing if he were a she wearing a revealing bikini bathing suit?"

I thought for a minute, then replied, "No, but that's different."

A New Trophy

Hilton Head Beach Services employs more than eighty lifeguards each summer to oversee twelve miles of oceanfront and keep the beachgoers safe. The responsibility of keeping the sands free of litter, however, rests with a much smaller cadre identified simply as the A.M. Beach Patrol.

The lifeguards are young, tanned, energetic college students. To help maintain their fitness, competitions are scheduled throughout the summer. These events attract appreciative crowds who cheer the lifeguards' athleticism.

The A.M. Beach Patrol corps, on the other hand, are old, retired folks, who go to bed early and, consequently, are up at 6:00 a.m. But it's hard to make trash picking competitive, so their efforts go mostly unnoticed. No one applauds when they stop to pick up a plastic cup.

And that is why I built a Trash Picker's Trophy, made of the typical stuff we cart to the dump each day. It isn't pretty, but it represents real life on the beach - beer bottles, potato chip bags, towels, etc. The memorial plaque reads simply, "In recognition of the dedicated men and women of the A.M. Beach Patrol who labor on the hot sands to keep our beaches clean." Rock on brave warriors.

Next I need to ensure it's given a place of honor in the life guards' trophy case. Bill's already gone on record as saying, "That's not going to happen."

But I take that as a challenge, too.

Forgotten Flowers

My partner Bill has good trash eyes. Better than mine. So he was the first to spot something floating by the water's edge, and we drove down to check it out.

"It's a bouquet of flowers," I said, as I carried them back to the truck. But it wasn't just any bouquet; it was a wedding bouquet with hundreds of small white flowers and tiny pearls woven together in an elaborate pattern.

"I bet this cost big bucks," I said. "What's it doing here in the water? I thought the bride was supposed to keep her flowers?"

"Maybe she decided not to get married," Bill offered matter-of-factly. "Maybe they had a beach wedding planned, and the groom was a no-show, and she got mad and tossed them into the ocean, or"... Bill continued, "Maybe they got married on a boat off shore and tossed the flowers overboard as part of the ceremony."

"Yeah, but the flowers haven't been in the salt water long, because they're still fresh", I added, trying not to let Bill take complete control of the investigation. "Here's what I think. I think they got married at sunrise on the beach, and the bride threw her bouquet to someone who didn't want to catch it because she didn't want to get married for some reason, and later that person disposed of the flowers quietly in the ocean."

Bill shook his head, "Too many someone's…too many loose ends."

We carefully placed the flowers in the back of the truck and spent the rest of the morning developing additional theories on the abandoned bouquet.

At the end of our shift, as we were headed for the dump, Bill motioned to the back seat and asked, "What do you want to do with those?"

"I don't know," I said. "I kept hoping all morning a woman in a white dress would appear from behind a sand dune, and claim her prize, but she didn't show."

Arch West

I didn't know Arch West and wouldn't recognize the man if I met him in Starbucks. But today, in his honor, I picked up an empty Doritos corn chip bag from the beach, tore off the label, and took it to the water's edge where I reverently placed it with the outgoing tide.

Arch West died this week at the age of ninety-seven. He was the snack food visionary responsible for introducing Doritos forty-nine years ago. His family plans to honor the man by sprinkling Doritos on his grave.

It reminds me of the Irishman, who, in preparation for his death, instructed a drinking buddy to pour a bottle of Irish whiskey over his grave to help ward off the evening chill. And the friend, thinking "What a waste of whiskey!" asked, "Do ya mind if I pass it through me kidneys first?"

Memorial Day

Today is Memorial Day and red, white and blue flags are everywhere. Before the day is over, the VFW will remind us that freedom isn't free, and the Marine Band will play God Bless America.

Six weeks from today, on July 4th, patriotism will be put on display again, and fireworks will light up the evening sky. Once again, hundreds of small American flags will dot the beaches of Hilton Head. But at the end of the day, patriotism gets left on the sands, and those flags lie stained and muddy, until eventually someone throws them in a trash barrel.

I'd rather pick up a hundred broken beer bottles, than sort through garbage to rescue a single, soiled American flag.

All Trash is not Created Equal

I'm going to let you in on a little secret. To the untrained eye, all rubbish on the beach looks the same. But to the professional, there are major differences.

For instance, happy trash is left over from a family picnic where everyone was having a good time, and forgot to pick up. It's a pail and shovel left on the beach by kids.

Bad trash is the nasty stuff like diapers and Band-Aids.

When beachgoers get stoned, break bottles and turn barrels over, that's mad trash. They deliberately create a mess.

So now you know the difference. All trash is not created equal, even if it looks the same on the sand. And happy trash is easier to pick up than mad trash.

Lifeguard Evaluation

A batch of new lifeguards started training today. Classroom stuff. The physical drills start later in the week. It's interesting how I subconsciously evaluate each lifeguard based on a single criterion. If I were drowning, and needed to be rescued, whom would I choose first?

The answer is always the biggest, muscular male guard on the beach. I wonder if it's a bias that has any statistical basis? Do petite female guards perform as well in emergencies when they're called upon to rescue someone twice their size?

Am I wrong to believe, in some situations, women are physically weaker? Does equality have to be an all-or-none proposition?

The Kazoo Band

She was the smallest of the children, yet trying desperately to lead the group. However, it was her clothing that really set her apart from the others. She was a kaleidoscope of colors: pink shirt, yellow shorts, red shoes and a green ribbon in her blond hair.

Holding her hand was an Asian boy, neatly dressed in black trousers and a white shirt. He was older and a foot taller. The two were swinging their arms in unison, while the bigger boy adjusted his stride to keep pace with his smaller partner.

Close behind them was a Hispanic girl wearing faded dungaree shorts, an African American with braided hair, and a pale skinny kid with his wrist in a plaster cast. The three were walking side by side with their arms entwined. The black girl was trying to coordinate their step, but not having much success. Another half dozen kids of various sizes and shapes followed. All were laughing.

Bringing up the rear was a chubby, freckled-faced youngster with a crew cut, pretending to play the drums. His head was thrown back, while his lips moved to an imaginary beat. He wore a shirt several sizes too small, spotted with perspiration.

They looked like a group put together by the United Nations, but they had one thing in common: they all had kazoos on strings around their necks. Some of the kids were playing tunes; some weren't. However, the songs varied. The result was a high-pitched, tinny rasp, but no one seemed to care.

Twenty yards back were three adults who were enjoying the parade as much as the kids. They, too, had kazoos. The oldest, a woman with braided gray hair, bib overalls and barn boots, was trying to high step, but having difficulty.

Bill and I watched as the parade approached, at which point I jumped out in front of the truck, and raising both arms shouted, "Stop. I have a request. Can you play *We Wish you a Merry Christmas"*?

A chorus came back "yes." The lady wearing barn boots scooted to the front to take charge, and the children's kazoo band attacked my request.

By now a small crowd of beachgoers had assembled. The band played several more songs. Then, as if it had been scripted, they broke into *God Bless America* and started moving down the beach. It was the finest rendition of that song I've ever heard, and that includes the original sung by Kate Smith.

I don't know who they were or why they were on the beach. I do believe that everyone who heard the children's kazoo band that morning was witness to one of life's special moments.

Don't Get Sucker Punched

After you've pulled trash on the beach for a while you become jaded. You think you've seen it all. Nothing surprises you anymore, and that's when you get sucker punched.

This morning as the sun was rising, I collected five pair of lacey thong panties from the sands of Coligny Beach: a red, black, yellow, blue and pink pair. They were arranged in a circle within a hundred feet of each other.

But wait there's more. I don't want you to get sucker punched like I was. In the middle of this panty circle was a large Vidalia onion.

Honest. I don't make this stuff up.

But wait- there's more. Don't get sucker punched twice. The Vidalia onion had a bite out of it. You could see the teeth marks.

Bill and I spent the rest of our shift speculating what could have gone on that night within the circle. Good taste prevents me from sharing our discussion with you, but I'm sure you have some of your own thoughts on this matter.

The Littlest Lifeguard

Adam is the lifeguard at chair #63. Standing on his toes he's 5'5"...maybe. And after six slices of pizza, and wearing a wet, sandy bathing suit, he might weigh 140 lbs. Adam is definitely the smallest male lifeguard on the beach. Half the female guards are taller and heavier than he is.

I've stated before: if I were drowning and needed to be rescued, I'd choose the biggest, most muscular male on the beach. However, in Adam's case, I'd make an exception.

Although he's only in his late teens, Adam displays a maturity not found in most of the guards. For instance, he listens to what you have to say before he speaks. He's not just quiet; he's listening. When he talks to a person, he makes direct eye contact. Adam is what my mother referred to as an "old soul" – someone who's lived more than one life, and with that experience is wise beyond his years.

Adam has modified his guard chair to fly an American flag. He's the only lifeguard who has. Each night he takes it down and folds it properly before securing his station. Adam is from Minnesota where he lives on a farm with nine older siblings. He claims he's the runt of the family. His Dad gave him the flag when Adam left for college. There's a story behind that gift I'm sure, but I haven't heard it yet. I just know if there were trouble on the beach, and you needed a little man with determination to do the right thing, I'd choose Adam every time.

Where Does the Trash Go?

It never fails. When the skies turn stormy, and thirty-knot gusts streak across the sands, the beach gets a magical face-lift. And when the winds eventually stop, the beach emerges polished and clean.

But sometimes I wonder: where does all that trash go? I don't think it gets blown out to sea. I believe it simply gets covered over. Think about that the next time you stretch out on the beach, and dig your toes into the soft, golden sand. And when the temperature in August hits one hundred degrees, and the faint aroma of garbage mingles with suntan oils, think about what's really down there decaying beneath the sands.

Apan Murica

"Do you need some help with that?" I called out the window of the red truck.

My offer was directed at a boy, no more than five, who was attempting to pull a wagon, filled with toys, onto the beach. However, he had hit a patch of soft sand, and the wagon was stuck.

Twenty feet behind him was a woman I guessed to be his mother. She was waging her own battle, juggling an assortment of stuff needed for a day at the beach. She nodded slightly, which I took as a signal it was okay to help. I picked up the wagon and carried it to a spot on the hard sand.

"There. This should be a good place to build sandcastles."

The boy smiled slightly, but did not speak.

He removed a plastic pail and shovel from the wagon and started digging. As he moved, I noticed one leg was shorter than the other.

While the mother unpacked the bags, the boy's attention shifted from castles to the red, white and blue dew rag I was wearing on my head. It was a patchwork of the American flag.

"Are you Apan Murica?" he asked.

"What?" I said, not understanding his words.

"Apan Murica," he repeated. "Are you Apan Murica?"

"He wants to know if you're Captain America," his mother interrupted. "You drove up in a red truck wearing an American flag headband. Captain America is one of his favorite super heroes."

I turned to the boy who was still staring up at me, and asked, "What's your name?"

"Icky," came the reply.

"His name is Ricky," his mother added quickly.

"No Ricky, I'm not Captain America," I said with a smile. "But I know where he lives. I'm his grandfather, and I'm going to tell him I met you today."

I went to the truck and retrieved a small American flag used for decoration on holidays.

"This is for your sand castle. Captain America would want you to have it."

Later that morning I went out of my way to revisit Ricky and his mother. I had collected several toy soldiers to give to my little superhero friend, but he was gone. All that remained was a castle, decorated with seashells, flying an American flag.

And in the hard sand someone had written "God Bless Captain America."

Formation Flying

If you've never been on the beach at dawn and witnessed a flock of brown pelicans fly a precision formation into the rising sun, add it to your bucket list. If you're lucky, you'll catch them on a flight where they've tucked into the trough of a curling wave, riding the air current.

The Navy's Blue Angels can't do it any better.

Lifeguard Saves Blind Dog

"No way," Bill said. "How'd she do that?"

"I don't know. Becky told me, and she didn't know either. She said Holly, the lifeguard at chair #38, rescued a blind dog yesterday."

"What's a blind dog doing in the ocean?" Bill continued. "They can't chase balls, or catch Frisbees. Was it swimming, or actually drowning?"

"Don't know," I repeated.

"I'll bet it was swimming," Bill concluded. "And if the dog was swimming, she really didn't rescue it."

"What if it was swimming out to sea?" I asked. "Don't forget the dog was blind."

Bill was silent for a moment as he considered several possibilities, and then asked, "Was it swimming out to sea?"

"I already told you, Bill, I don't know."

The next morning Bill was all smiles as he announced, "Well Mister know-it-all, I checked with Becky and, as usual, you had the story all wrong. The dog wasn't blind. It was deaf."

No Speak the English

Yesterday I picked up a discarded instructional booklet for assembling a new beach umbrella. Curious to find out why it was a half-inch thick, I started thumbing through the pages. There were French, Spanish, Chinese, and Japanese sections. There were even instructions in a language I didn't recognize. However, the real shocker came when I discovered the English section was only two pages.

Can I conclude that's because the average American is intelligent enough to assemble a beach umbrella without instructions? Or are there more serious implications here regarding the future of the English language?

Mouthwash

On a typical four-hour shift, Bill and I stop twice at a men's room. That, of course, assumes we confine our morning coffee intake to no more than two cups. Today, at the Marriot Hotel stop, several changes were evident in the men's facility next to the pool. The soap dispensers were full of a new, fragrant soap, and a variety of hair shampoos and conditioners were neatly arranged on a ceramic tray. There were even bottles of minty mouthwash.

"Is this for us?" I asked Bill.

"I don't think so," was his reply. "They have a new spa, and this is probably one of the ways they intend to promote it." Bill picked up a tiny mouthwash bottle, opened it, and took a long swig.

"Hey this tastes pretty good," he said, swishing the liquid around in his mouth. "You can kiss me now."

Unfortunately, Bill's back was to the door as he made this loving declaration, and he did not see or hear the two vacationers who had just entered.

It's been almost a week now, and Bill has refused to stop at the Marriot until he's positive those guys have checked out.

Trying to Forget

His head was down as he shuffled towards us. Bill slowed the red truck to a crawl, and it was then I noticed he was reading a letter. He would have walked into the front of the truck if Bill hadn't blown the horn. Startled, he looked up and shook his head. He was crying.

"Sorry," Bill called out the window as we passed.

There was no reply.

Later that morning we saw the man again, sitting with a small boy who was digging in the sand. The man was pouring water from a pail into the hole the boy had made. Both were smiling.

People usually come to the beach to relax and have a good time.

Sometimes, however, they come to forget.

Camilla

Juan looks more like a line backer than a lifeguard. His broad muscular upper body and flat tight stomach suggest hours spent in a weight room.   And although Juan has an Adonis body most men covet and most women dream of, it's not what you notice first when you see him on the beach.   On the back of his shoulder Juan has a life sized tattoo of a beautiful woman's face, beneath which is inscribed: Camilla 12/15/1986 - 4/7/2009.

I asked another lifeguard who the woman was. She shook her head, stating that she had only heard rumors. One was that it was his wife; the other that it was an older sister.

"Does anyone know how she died?" I asked, seeking more information.

"No," was the reply. "Juan doesn't hang out with any of the other lifeguards. He does his beach shift and goes home. He's a great looking guy, but it's sad. He never smiles."

Found on the Beach

This weekend a tropical storm visited the island. 45 mph winds blasted the sand, scattered trash barrels, and roughed up the surf. At times like this we always find interesting stuff half buried in the sand.

Today it was a silver-plated butter knife and a plastic laminated card showing the emergency exits of an American Airlines DC-10.

Found on the Beach Part 2

I nearly ran over it with the truck, except a ray of sunshine reflected off its shiny, white surface. It was low tide, and the curved, plastic lip protruded several inches above the flat sand. I had no idea what it was, but knew an injury could result if someone struck it with a bare foot. I got the shovel from the trailer and started digging. Bill watched with amusement, occasionally offering advice.

I dug, then squatted down and pulled, then dug and tugged some more, but the mysterious object was unyielding. Fifteen minutes later I had worked up a sweat digging a rather large hole, but was still clueless as to what I was attempting to unearth... just that it was white, made of plastic, and had an oval shape.

Finally Bill brought an end to the exercise by shouting, "Okay, enough is enough. Get the tow chain from the trunk." A few minutes later the puzzle was solved, and Bill was taking a picture of me holding a toilet seat, complete with cover, while leaning proudly on my shovel.

What's That Smell?

"Does this truck smell musty?" Bill asked, as he looked around the cab interior for a possible cause.

I took a sniff and answered cautiously, "I don't smell anything."

"Well I do," Bill snapped. "Something has been smelling bad all week, and it's getting worse."

I quickly changed the subject, but when I got home I took off my sneakers and stuck them under my nose. My head recoiled as I fought back an involuntary gag. Bill's use of the adjective "musty" to describe the odor had been kind. I washed the shoes with laundry soap under the garden hose, and the following morning, while they were still wet, applied a liberal application of Dr. Scholl's foot powder.

Once again I performed the sniff test. The musty smell was gone, but the rancid odor that remained was not much of an improvement. Then I remembered once in college using aftershave lotion in my running shoes to solve a similar problem. I found a bottle of Old Spice, and sprinkled it over the Dr. Scholl's. Another sniff. The musty smell was gone.

That morning I arrived early and was waiting as Bill entered the truck. It didn't take long.

"What's going on here?" he shouted. "It's you, isn't it? That smell is coming from you."

"It's my sneakers, Bill," I confessed.

"I knew it," he cried. "Take them off, and put them in the trailer. They're even worse than yesterday. What did you do to them? It smells like someone puked in a lilac bush."

Missing Morals

The notice on the Beach Services bulletin board this morning read: Lost or Stolen - Greg's Moral Compass. If found please return to…
There was a name and number.

I don't know Greg. I assume he's one of the new lifeguards, and I'm sorry to learn his compass is missing.

My Aunt was fond of quoting Bertrand Russell who once said, "There are two kinds of morality. One, which we preach, but do not practice; and another, which we practice, but seldom preach.

I hope Greg is able to recover his moral compass, but I don't believe it was stolen. Either he lost it, or gave it away.

Dead or Alive

It was partially hidden between two clumps of seaweed, but it looked as if it might be alive. So I tapped it with the toe of my shoe. It quivered, and I retreated a step.

"Hey, Bill, come here and look at this," I called.

I brushed some more seaweed aside. It looked like brain coral, except the membrane was not boney. It was flesh-like and pinkish. I remember as a child going to the butcher's shop with my mother where she would occasionally buy tripe. Tripe comes from the cow's stomach, and although some consider it a delicacy, it was a meal I vowed would never pass my lips. This looked like tripe.

"What do you think it is?" I asked.

"No idea," Bill answered curtly.

"Do you think it'd dead or alive?

Bill shrugged his shoulders. He was losing patience. "And don't tell me you want to dig this up."

I was quiet as I gazed down at the mystery object, then turned and headed for the truck. "Bill, you have no intellectual curiosity," I shouted over my shoulder.

I wasn't going to remind him that I once dug up a toilet seat.

Bad Advice

The message, written in the sand, read: Never Be Afraid.

"What kind of advice is that?" I asked. "Everyone's afraid at one time or another. It's normal. Fear's a healthy thing. "

"Maybe they're talking about the positive effects of overcoming your fears," Bill suggested thoughtfully.

"Well they didn't say that," I countered.

Bill was silent for a moment, and then said, "A cat bitten once by a snake, fears even a rope."

I thought for a moment. "Oh yeah...well remember: fear is temporary; pride is forever."

And so it continued. Before the morning shift was over, we had punished each other by reciting every fear quote or platitude we could remember.

Lost and Found

The five barrels were lined in a row, but only one had trash in it. Perched on top of the pile was a pair of sandals. They were in good condition, and as I lifted them up I noticed that tucked inside one shoe was a black sock filed with personal items: cigarettes, a lighter, a smart phone, an expensive watch, a package of condoms, a driver's license, and in the bottom, a wad of Andrew Jackson bills rolled in a rubber band. I counted four-hundred dollars.

When our shift ended we turned all the loot over to Becky who runs Lost and Found for Beach Services. She was able to locate the owner who came in that afternoon and claimed his stuff.

"Did he at least say thank you?" I asked the next day.

"Why? For returning his condoms?" Becky said with a smile. "He was quick to count his money though. It looked like he was still recovering from last night's party."

"Oh, you mean we might find his wallet again tomorrow," I said sarcastically.

Alligators on the Beach

Hilton Head Island is dotted with hundreds of fresh water lagoons. Local realtors market these mud puddles as island amenities, but their real purpose is to hide a growing alligator population. Most gators, because they are territorial creatures, spend their entire life in the same neighborhood lagoon.

But today's newspaper had a story about a thirteen-foot rogue alligator that was frightening visitors in a local park. Finally, after it swallowed some kid's soccer ball, Critter Management was called in. Apparently a crock this size cannot be relocated, so it's harvested and the proceeds distributed to local food banks.

The article then described in great detail what was found in the giant lizard's belly. It was a smorgasbord of tasty snacks: 53 fishing lures, 48 rocks, 2 turtles, 2 baseballs, a tennis ball, ½ lb. of lead sinkers, and an unopened beer can. In addition, mixed in with other partially digested stuff, was the main entrée – another four-foot gator. Further proof, if such is needed, that these creatures are territorial.

Bill told me that every couple of years a sick alligator ends up on our beaches. He claims that, when a crock becomes infected with parasites, it's not unusual for them to seek a salt-water bath for the illness.

I can only imagine the shrieks from the guests at the Westin Hotel, if they ever discovered a thirteen-foot scaly amphibian next to them under a blue beach umbrella.

First Aid for Poopsie

"Looks like trouble," I said to Bill, as I gazed out the windshield of the red truck. A hundred yards ahead an overweight woman, clad in a clingy, black bathing suit and wearing an oversized straw hat, was frantically jumping up and down. Cradled tightly in one fleshly arm was a small, shaggy dog yapping excitedly.

"Stop...stop," she called as we approached. "Poopsie's been stung by a jelly fish."

"This one's yours," Bill whispered. "Tend to the needs of your flock. I'll observe from the truck."

"Thanks," I muttered as I got the vinegar solution bottle from the trailer. "I owe you."

"What's that?" the woman asked eying the bottle as I approached. "It won't hurt him, will it?"

"No ma'am. It'll just relieve the sting. Do you know where he was stung?"

"On the nose. He was sniffing one of those horrible jelly creatures down by the water," she said pointing.

I started to explain that those were dead jellyfish and had lost their sting capability, but Poopsie's bark had now become a low growl. I looked back at the truck for assistance, but Bill had managed to hide himself from view.

"Is there a hospital nearby where we can have Poopsie treated?" the lady in black asked.

I disregarded the inference in her question regarding my first aid skills, and replied, "I don't think that's necessary ma'am. Cover his eyes and I'll spray his nose with this prescription used specifically for jelly stings."

She must have misunderstood my instructions, because instead of covering the dog's eyes with her hand, the lady closed her own eyes. I didn't care. I positioned the bottle a few inches from Poopsie's nose. He growled louder, and then sniffed the nozzle. I pulled the trigger once…then twice more for good measure. The dog stopped growling, and the lady opened her eyes.

"Oh my…is he okay?" she asked, pushing her large, pale face within inches of Poopsie's, and kissing his wet nose.

"Good as new," I said, surprised to learn that the vinegar and water solution worked so well on dogs. As she was thanking me, she bent down and placed Poopsie at her feet. Immediately the dog took off for the water, and the woman realized he was headed back for the jellyfish.

"Poopsie…Come back here", she cried, as I retreated to the red truck.

"Go…go," I shouted at Bill, who was now back in the driver's seat shaking his head and laughing.

The 4th of July

Yesterday was the 4th of July, and around the island there were lots of fireworks. In fact, at ten o'clock last night, I stopped at Burke's Beach and simultaneously watched parts of three different shows. It was enjoyable. But this morning, firework remnants littered the beach.

I guess with every celebration there's a cleanup involved – whether it's a barbeque, or a wedding, or even a simple dinner. A fireworks display is no different. But still I wonder: How does South Carolina justify the legality of selling fireworks, while maintaining it's illegal to discharge them?

Bill has a simple explanation. The State wants visitors to spend their money here, load the fireworks in the trunks of their cars, drive home, and light them off. Let someone else worry about the safety issues and cleanup.

What Were They Thinking

A filler piece in the Island Packet newspaper caught my attention this morning. It was originally reported in the South Florida Sun-Sentinel. Tom Lopez, a lifeguard, was fired after leaving his post to rescue a swimmer outside his designated area. The Associated Press quickly took the story national when four other lifeguards protested the action and resigned in support of Lopez. The same day the Mayor piled on the controversy by stating, "It has always been the city's policy that a lifeguard must respond to an emergency inside or outside of their protected area." The drowning victim added his support by heaping praise on his rescuer.

With the internet airwaves humming support for Lopez, the story finally ended when the head of the management company publicly apologized stating: "The lifeguard had been fired too quickly, but that no area of the beach had been left unattended while Lopez went to assist a distressed swimmer."

However, the story didn't officially end until the fired lifeguard was interviewed on national television and stated he didn't want his job back.

What were they thinking?

"Is that what I think it is?" Bill scowled looking out the truck window.

"What?" I asked, trying to follow his gaze. I had no idea what he was looking at.

"Propped on top of that trash barrel in front of the Westin Hotel."

I squinted at the line of barrels two hundred yards ahead. "That thing in the middle? It looks like one of those small hotel refrigerators," I guessed

"No it doesn't. Are you blind? It's got a picture screen. It's a television," Bill concluded as he stopped the truck next to the barrel.

"Who brings a television like that to the beach?" I asked, getting out for a closer look. "This looks like the set we had when I was a kid. Except ours had rabbit ears."

The TV was vintage. It only had three adjustable knobs, two of which were missing. The channel knob was etched with the numbers 2, 4, 6, and 7.

"I think I watched Howdy Dowdy on Channel 2," Bill recalled.

"Yeah" I said remembering the show fondly. "But it didn't come on until 4:00 p.m., so you'd stare at a test pattern until you heard Buffalo Bob shouting 'Hey kids, what time is it?' This set has to be at least fifty years old."

"Closer to sixty," Bill countered. "Do you think it still works? Say, here's an idea. Why don't you take it home to the Mrs. and tell her you'd like to put it in the living room."

We loaded the old memory box into the trailer, and for the rest of our shift played "Do You Remember."

"What show came on after Howdy Dowdy?"

"Captain Kangaroo."

"No…No, You're crazy. It was Kukla Fran and Ollie."

"I never liked that show."

"Me neither, but it was better than staring at a test pattern."

A Sick Day

I called in sick today. That rarely happens. I know Bill was surprised.

"You sound terrible," he said. "Have you seen a doctor?"

"No. I'll be okay tomorrow," I moaned. My head was throbbing, my throat was sore, and I knew I had a fever.

I can't remember the last time I missed a day of work due to illness. My life has been blessed with good heath, but I also have a high tolerance for pain, which I inherited from my father. He suffered for thirty years with rheumatoid arthritis, yet managed to regularly clock fifty-hour workweeks and never complained.

In a masochistic way I sometimes welcome a bad toothache. My wife shakes her head whenever I refer to pain as the ultimate character builder.

Bill called later to see how I was feeling.

"I'm better," I said. "Don't worry, I'll be ready for duty tomorrow." When I hung up the phone I thought again about my father and the many life lessons I learned from him.

He was my hero.

The Tourist

He was in his late thirties, short, with a potbelly. He had a mop of ruffled, red hair and was wearing a faded sweatshirt that proclaimed, "Life is Good."

"Howdy," he said approaching the truck. "Sure is a pretty day, ain't it?"

Not waiting for an answer, he continued, "We don't have anything like this in Kentucky. No sir, we sure don't." He looked around the beach, and then out at the ocean. "This water sure does move around a lot, don't it? When I was down here early this morning it was way out there." He pointed. "Now it's way up here."

"That's because the tide's coming in," Bill said, trying to make polite conversation. "It will be high in another hour, and then low six hours after that."

"Well I'll be. Don't that just beat all," drawled our Kentucky friend. "How many of these tides y'all have here each day anyway?"

And with a straight face, Bill replied, "Two."

Dog Groupies

We know lots of people who walk the beach regularly, but we can only identify them by their dogs. There's Jake, Harley, Carolina, Muffin, Wolf, Cashew, Sadie, and a dozen others. Bill's a canine lover, and has been feeding some of these dogs for years. Long before I arrived on the scene. As a result, it's not unusual to have a dog start chasing the red truck as soon as it comes in to view. To them it represents a dog biscuit.

What is surprising, there are five other identical trucks that patrol the beach, and the dogs pay little attention to them. Our trailer is identified only with the #6, and many pet owners insist their dog will only chase #6.

It's hard for me to believe the dogs are able to identify the only truck on the beach with a supply of treats.

But as they say, truth is often stranger than fiction.

The Best Job in the World

I had just swung the heavy trash bag up and over the side of the trailer when I heard a voice from behind say, "You've got the best job in the whole world."

"And what makes you say that?" I asked, turning to confront my admirer.

She was in her late 30's, pretty in a bright yellow bathing suit, while balancing a baby on one shapely hip.

She flashed a dazzling white smile. "Well at least that's what my husband says. He wants your job when he retires," she added.

"He does?" I said, trying to return her smile, but immediately aware I was flirting with Ms. Pepsodent Toothpaste. I closed my mouth and ran my tongue over my teeth, trying to remember if I had even brushed this morning.

"Yes, he says you're performing a service that makes a difference. But equally important, you're on the beach at sunrise, the most beautiful time of the day, and you're your own boss, and there's no stress involved."

"You also meet a lot of interesting people," I added, putting emphasis on the word "interesting". I didn't want the conversation to end. If Bill had backed the truck over my foot at this point, I may not have felt a thing.

And then a male voice, from behind a nearby beach umbrella, broke the spell.

My Performance Review

When I arrived at work today, Bill was standing in front of the truck. He had a stern look on his face, and his hands were hidden behind his back. As I approached he announced in a deep voice, "Do you know what day this is?"

I thought for a moment and replied, "Wednesday."

"No," he corrected. "It's your anniversary. You've been a member of the A.M. Trash Patrol for three years today…"

I started to say, "My how time flies."

But Bill interrupted, "… and in recognition of your performance, we at Beach Services wish to present you with this token of our gratitude."

He took his hands from behind his back and held out a wristwatch. It was made of black plastic, and had a rusted metal clasp. Bits of sand still clung to the strap. As Bill attempted to place the watch on my wrist, I noticed it had no face and no inner mechanism.

"It's very nice, Bill, and I'm moved by your thoughtfulness. But how am I supposed to tell time with this?" I pointed to the hole where the watch dial and workings had been.

"Ah yes…those," he mused. "Those come on your fifth anniversary. Keep up the good work, Corporal." And with that, he saluted, did an awkward about face, and climbed into the red truck.

"Oh well," I thought as I stared at what had been strapped on my wrist. "Only two more years to go."

Explain it to me

It's late September, and it's quiet on the beach. The joggers and dog walkers are still here, but most of the tourists have gone. It rained all night, so there were no beach parties. We only collected two bags of trash this morning but still managed to accumulate a dozen beach chairs.

"How can that be," I said to Bill as he tossed the last chair into the trailer. "There's practically no one on the beach to generate trash, yet we still gather all these chairs. Explain to me, old wise one," I continued, "How can this be?"

And Bill, in an all knowing authoritative voice explained, "Things are not always as they appear, my son. What you believe to be a beach chair, may not indeed be one. It may be the spirit of the brown pelican clouding your eyes and making you ..."

"Okay...okay," I interrupted. "Just a simple 'I don't know' will suffice."

She started waving her arms as I approached.

"Stop, please...Stop," I heard her cry.

She was a small woman, less than five feet, but weighed close to three hundred pounds. A red bathing suit, still wet from the ocean, clung to her round body.

"Do you have any stuff for jelly fish stings?" she asked, pointing to the back of the truck.

"Yes ma'am," I replied, retrieving the water and vinegar bottle. "Where have you been stung?"

"If you don't mind," she said, "it's personal." Before I could ask another question she grabbed the bottle from my hand, spun around so her back was to me, and yanked down the top of her bathing suit. Then she began spraying her ample chest.

"Oh yes, that's better," she moaned.

When she finished, she turned again, and with a flirtatious smile thanked me for being a gentleman. I blushed.

Later that day, when I told Bill the story, we wondered how the jellyfish managed to navigate in and out of such a tight space.

The Septic Stick

I was fifteen minutes late for work today. Bill was waiting in the red truck, listening to the news on PBS radio.

"I cut myself shaving", I said, pointing to the wad of toilet paper hanging from the right side of my chin.

"So I see," Bill acknowledged, staring at the crimson pad of dried blood. "How'd you do that?"

"I used my wife's razor," I admitted. "I'm not used to five blades; mine only has two. Then I couldn't find a septic stick."

"A what?" Bill mused with a grin.

"A septic stick."

"I haven't seen one of those since high school. Do they still make them," Bill asked, the smile spreading across his face.

"I hope so, because I need a new one. I don't know what happened to the one I had."

"Get in the truck," Bill instructed, shaking his head in disbelief. "Maybe you'll get lucky and find one on the beach. By the way, I think they're called styptic pencils, not septic sticks. I don't want you to embarrass yourself if you try to buy one in Walgreen's."

Mr. Fix It

Today is Saturday. It's my day off. Yet here I am on the beach riding my fat tire bike. I just met an old friend I haven't seen in a year. Mike is working part time for a vacation rental company – one that specializes in the multi-million dollar mansions that dot the shoreline. Houses with swimming pools and great views of the ocean rent for more than $10,000 a week. Mike works as a level one handyman. When a family checks in and finds the toaster doesn't pop up or the toilet doesn't flush properly, he's the guy the rental company sends out to fix it.

"The company pays me $14 an hour, and if I can't solve the problem, they get a professional who charges $80. It's a good deal for everyone," Mike explained. "I'll bet you can't guess what I get called for the most?"

I shook my head.

"The television set," he said. "Someone can't get their favorite show or channel, or can't operate the remote control, and they get upset. Here they are spending ten grand for an ocean front house, and their first concern is the TV. Can you believe that?"

"Yeah. Unfortunately, I can," I replied.

Mike sighed. "If you want to know what God thinks of money, just look at the people he gave it to."

Changes in Retirement

The day I retired from my job on Wall Street, I took off my wristwatch. It was a symbolic gesture. I hoped it would magically free me from the afflictions built up over forty years when my life was controlled by the hands of the clock. It didn't. I found myself looking at my bare wrist a lot. Old habits die slowly.

Life's much simpler on beach patrol. I only need to know if the tide's coming in or going out. And I can't start collecting trash before sunrise, because it's too dark.

I don't need a watch for that.

The Weather for Today is...

The weather forecast today, according to The Island Packet, is "Partly Cloudy." Whether it's partly cloudy, or partly sunny, is up to the individual. As for me, it's always sunny on the beach

A New Day

It was dark when red truck #6 rolled to a stop on the sand. Sunrise would not be for another ten minutes. Bill turned off the motor, and the world was still. We sipped our coffee and waited as the curtain of darkness slowly lifted on a new day.

A ghost crab, heading for home, paused briefly to make sure it wasn't being followed, and then disappeared beneath the sand. A young white egret, still learning to fish, waited patiently by the water's edge. Thirty feet offshore a mother dolphin with her baby maneuvered behind a school of baitfish. A shrimp boat, with both outriggers extended, pitched gently in a following sea. The rhythmic chug-chug of its diesel engine was mixed with the piercing squawk of the gulls fighting for position above the nets.

Dawn finally arrived. It was October 1st, our last day with Beach Services until next season. Bill started the truck. For we had miles to go before we sleep and trash to sweep to earn our keep.